pirates sale the seas but not all
pirates make it out alive.

BOOK 1

Once in a world were creatures thrive technology is blue magic is big and of course pirates stealing treasure getting to the bottom of the seas and there was one pirate of them all clancino who was the best in

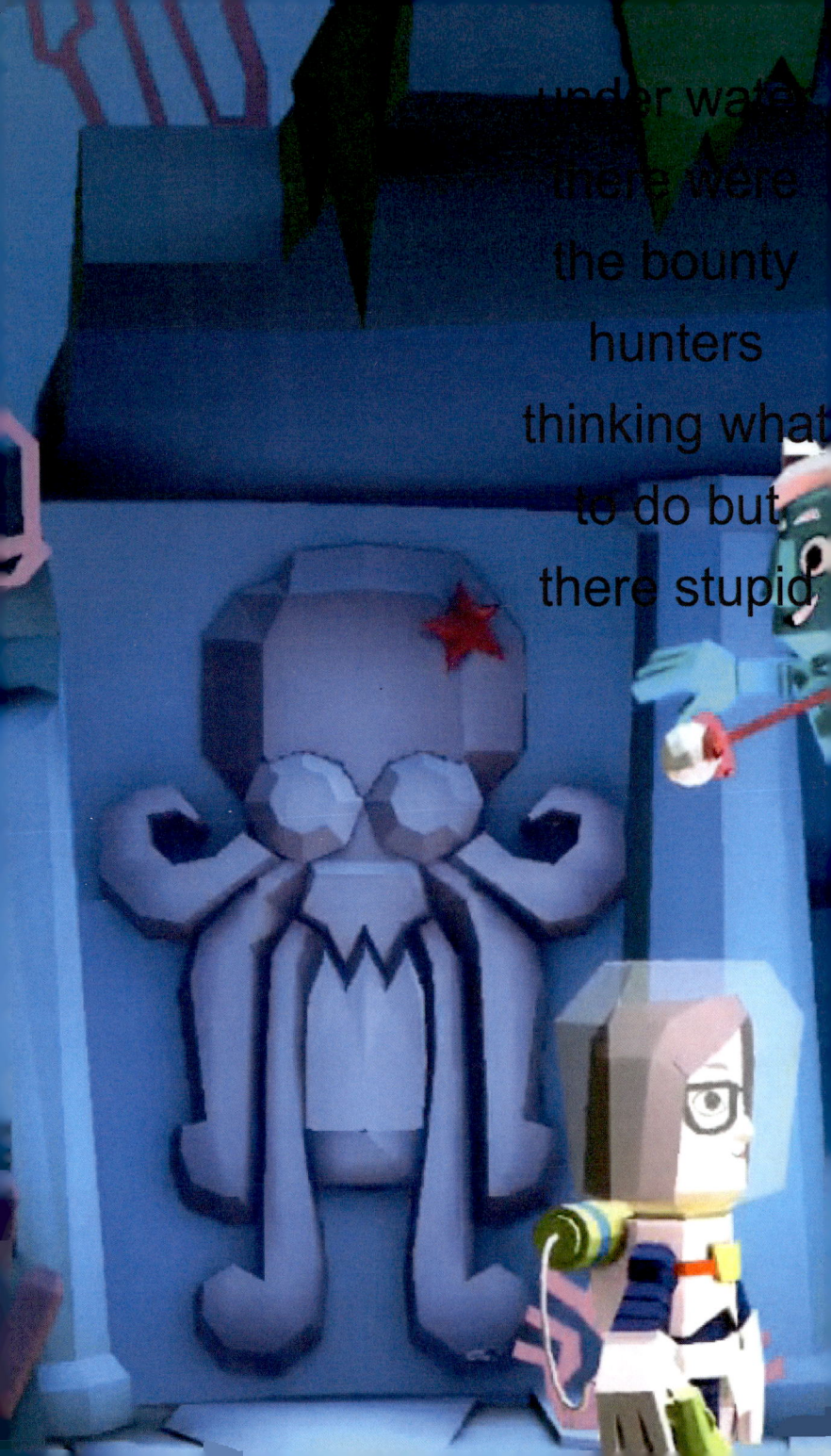

clancho got capture put inside a lazer vault he couldn't get ou but one day th hunter was there and

general and bounty were thinking when they had an idea use that machine and he would become the claneral/

This book is based on a youtube series this book is a multi part book this is episode 1 this book is of season 1.

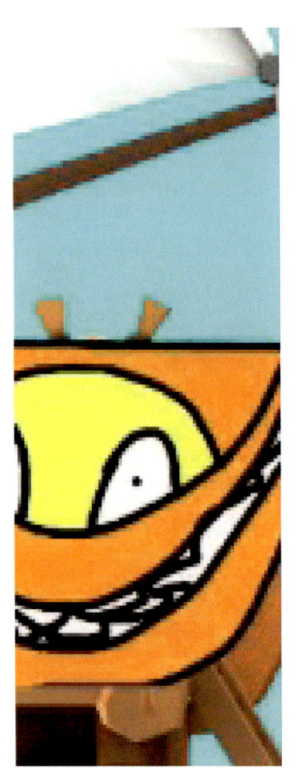